JUST WILLIAM'S

PUZZLES

AN OUTLAWS CLUB BOOK

featuring
Richmal Crompton's
Just – William
and
the Outlaws

M

MACMILLAN CHILDREN'S BOOKS

First published 1994 by
Macmillan Children's Books
a division of Macmillan General Books Ltd
Cavaye Place London SW10 9PG
and Basingstoke

Associated companies throughout the world

ISBN 0 333 62680 X
Copyright © Macmillan Children's Books

Text and illustrations by David Mostyn.
The illustrations are inspired by the original pictures by
Thomas Henry and are published by permission of the
Thomas Henry Estate.
William and the Outlaws appear in the William Books
© Richmal Crompton and Richmal Ashbee.

9 8 7 6 5 4 3 2 1

A CIP catalogue record for this book is available from
the British Library.

Printed and bound in Great Britain by
BPC Hazell Books Ltd

important mesege

Ive ritten this bok so you have something to do
when its boring at school or wen your
mother wants you to clear up your room
or wen grown ups want you to be quiet.

They are jolly interesting puzzels but if your
not braney enough to know all the ansers
then you will find them at the end of the
bok. I no all the ansers of corse.

(Signed) William Brown
Alas the Black Hand

The Outlaws ESCAPE

William, Henry, Douglas and Ginger have almost been trapped into playing dolls with Violet Elizabeth Bott. By running down the right paths they can escape to safety in the old barn. Can you find the right way for them to go?

William finds hidden Treasure

While the Outlaws were playing in an old house, William found an old map under some floor-boards. Is it a hidden treasure map? Hunt for the treasure yourselves.

T	M	A	P	U	V	O	T	S	N	I	O	C	A
F	A	Z	R	R	B	P	V	A	V	P	A	Z	S
W	E	U	Q	S	E	D	U	B	L	O	O	N	S
G	Y	A	T	P	G	H	R	I	W	R	C	T	T
H	D	I	A	M	O	N	D	S	T	S	E	G	V
P	B	B	S	I	L	V	E	R	P	N	G	O	X
D	V	C	X	Y	J	K	S	T	F	O	J	B	Z
I	W	M	L	O	N	L	U	S	G	I	K	L	B
O	N	D	L	O	G	M	L	E	J	L	M	E	C
Y	B	C	I	J	K	E	V	N	A	L	N	T	D
I	Z	X	A	D	W	F	E	P	T	U	P	S	F
H	C	D	G	E	T	F	G	O	V	B	R	H	P
K	A	B	J	V	R	S	U	Q	R	V	T	Z	T

GOLD   JEWELS   DUBLOONS
SILVER   COINS   GOBLETS
BULLION   DIAMONDS   MAP

Ginger Helps Out

Ginger, with the aid of the Outlaws, has helped unload the coal. But he has put it in a place that his mother will not be very happy about. Where did he put it?

1
• 4×2

$\frac{4}{2}$

$\frac{6}{2}$
•

10-3
•

$\frac{8}{2}$
•

2×3 $\frac{10}{2}$
•   ••

25-2

3×3
•

• 6×2

10   12-1
•   •

11×2 •
        • 3×7

20-7   9×2 •
•   •

• 8×2   20-3 30-11 5×4
2×7•   •   ••

• 3×5

the Very odd Monster

The Outlaws have found the tracks of lots of terrible monster animals. Which tracks are the odd ones out?

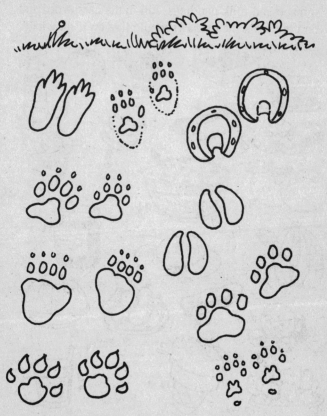

William the Cook

If William and the Outlaws had their way, they would never cook any dull food like prunes and spinach and milk puddings. Fill in the crossword and find out what the Outlaws would live on if they had their way.

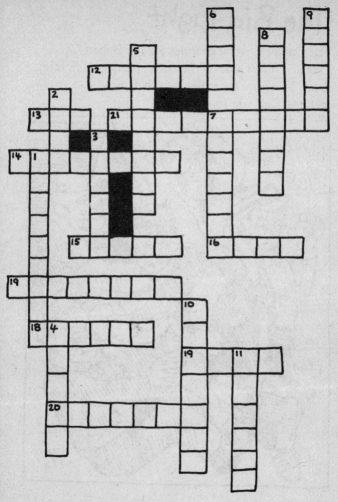

The Big Fight

The Outlaws' worst enemies are the Hubert Laneites. The Outlaws' favourite pastime is fighting them. There are ten differences between these two pictures. Can you spot them?

the Midnight Feast

Douglas' parents are out for the evening and he has invited the rest of the Outlaws round to his house for a midnight binge. Which of the six pictures is the correct 'negative' picture of the big scene?

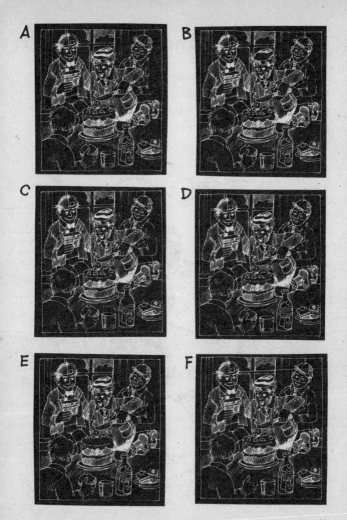

The Outlaws and the Big Catch

William, Henry, Douglas and Ginger have gone fishing. One of the Outlaws has caught a really big fish. The other Outlaws have tried to help him, but their lines have become entangled. Which Outlaw has caught the fish?

The Fancy Dress Party

William has been invited to a dull and boring fancy dress party. But when he gets there he notices something very funny. Some of the children are wearing the same costumes. Can you see how many pairs of children are wearing the same thing?

Detention

Ginger will be kept in after school if he can't finish these sums in two minutes. Can you help him?

$$20 + 25 =$$

$$7324 - 7279 =$$

$$15 \times 3 =$$

$$276 \div 6 =$$

SWEEPING the CHIMNEY

The sweep has come to clean the chimneys at Ginger's house. While he is having tea in the kitchen the Outlaws decide to sweep a chimney to help him out. Which five rods, connected together, will reach to the top of a twelve metre chimney?

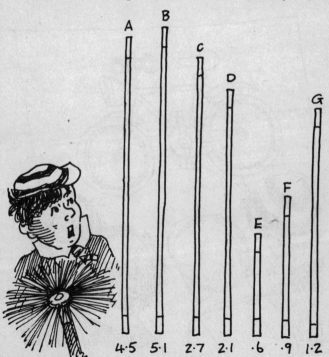

A B C D E F G

4·5 5·1 2·7 2·1 ·6 ·9 1·2

19

The Outlaws Build a Bike

Henry, Douglas, Ginger and of course, William, have found four boxes of old bicycle parts. They want to build a bike, but only one of the four boxes has all the correct parts. Match the contents of one of the boxes to the plan that the Outlaws have found.

OutLaw Band

William and the Outlaws have formed a band. Can you find all their instruments?

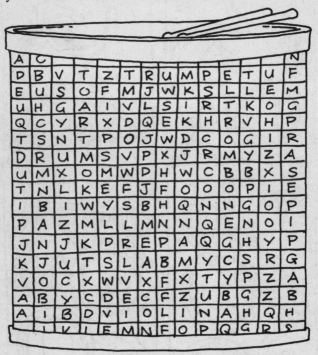

DRUM VIOLIN BAGPIPES

CYMBALS BANJO TRUMPET

TROMBONE SAXOPHONE

DEADLY ENEMIES

Some of William's most deadly enemies are hiding
in the bushes. Find them before William does.

GEORGIE   TEACHERS
HUBERT   ROBERT
ETHEL   FATHER
MRS BOTT   BERTIE

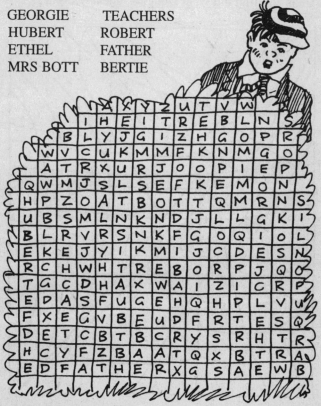

DouglAS AND THE GhoST

Douglas insists he has seen a ghost. The other Outlaws don't believe him. Can you fill in the dotted areas and find out what Douglas' ghost really is?

THe Hidden WeAPoNS

William and his gang have captured the Hubert
Laneites weapons, and hidden them. Can you find
all six of them?

WilLiAM THE DETECTiVE

William has found a mysterious footprint in the flower bed. He has lined up all the shoes he can find and is trying to work out which shoes match the print in the flower bed. Can you find the matching shoe?

The Outlaws' Favourite Things

Find out what William and the Outlaws really like best.

The Go-KART

William, Henry, Douglas, and Ginger have built a wonderful go-kart, and the Hubert Laneites want to capture it. Which path should William take to avoid capture?

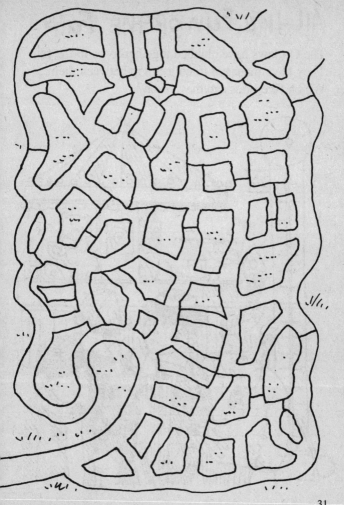

All the Fun of the Fair

The Outlaws have clubbed together to go to the fair.
They have managed to collect 85p between them.
Which five rides can they go on?

33

WHAT A TREAT!

The Outlaws have seen something they like more than anything else. What is it?

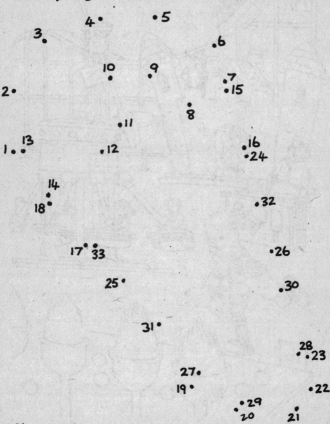

Greedy Hubert

Ginger has a clever trick and Hubert Lane is
desperate to find the answer, because Ginger has
promised to give Hubert a chocolate if he can
solve the puzzle. Can you do it?

Bathing Jumble

William has invited the Outlaws to his house to wash Jumble who is looking very dirty. Each Outlaw has his own hose-pipe, and things get a bit confused. Which Outlaw ends up washing Jumble?

NEver Play with Matches

It was a rotten rainy day, and William was very bored. When he asked if he could play with some matches, his mother gave him the matches, but took away the box! Luckily, the Browns had a cousin staying and he showed William a clever trick. All William had to do was to move one match to get the sum right. How did he do it?

FOREIGNERS !

William has a relative staying at his house. He is a mad scientist and William can't understand what he is talking about. Can you understand?

" SOWIN WDOOC LHHT ! "

Down with School

The Outlaws didn't like school at all. Here are a few things that they wished had never been invented.

$$\frac{3926}{7} \times 3 =$$

$$17 \div 5 \times 2 =$$

$$a + b^2(a^2 \times b^2) = xy^2 \times ab^2(xy^2)$$

FIND THE HIDDEN WORD

RED Rag to A Bull

The Outlaws are in a sticky situation. Unless they can get out of the field quickly, either the bull or the angry farmer is going to catch them. Can you find the way out?

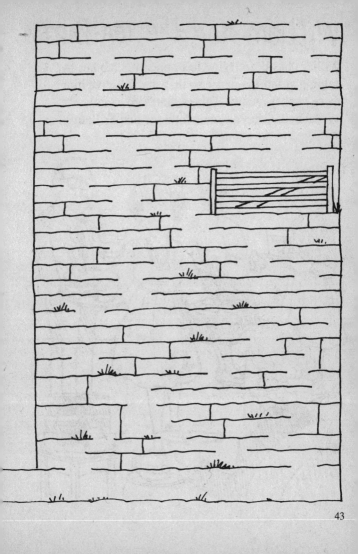

William and the TEA-PARTY

William has been trying to impress his mother by helping at her tea-party, so that she will give him more pocket-money. Things didn't go exactly as planned. Can you see ten things that William managed to do wrong?

SNoW-BaLL fiGHT

It's been snowing, which as far as the Outlaws are concerned, is a perfect opportunity for a fight with the Laneites. How many snowballs can you see?

Sinister Stranger

The Outlaws have seen a sinister person at the window of an old disused house. Each of them has drawn a picture of what he thinks the stranger looked like. Which is the correct drawing of the shape in the window?

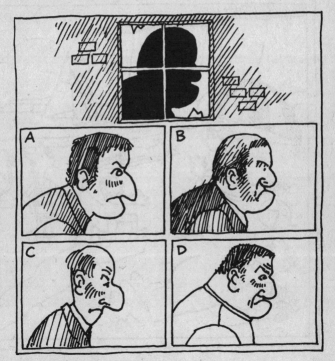

WiLLiAM The Photographer

William has been on holiday and is proudly showing off his photographs to the rest of the Outlaws. But Douglas has seen some things that are a bit strange in one of the pictures. Can you see all 10 things?

tHE Outlaws' BARN

The old barn is the Outlaws' Headquarters. But the awful Hubert Lane and his gang have got in and messed the place up. Can you spot the differences between how the barn should look, and how it looks when the Laneites have been there?

Henry's Disguise

Henry is in disguise and the rest of the Outlaws are admiring him in the mirror. Which picture is the right mirror image of Henry?

tHE HiSTORY LESSON

The Outlaws like history lessons because of all the fighting. Henry has drawn his favourite historical object on the black board. Shade in the dotted areas. What is it?

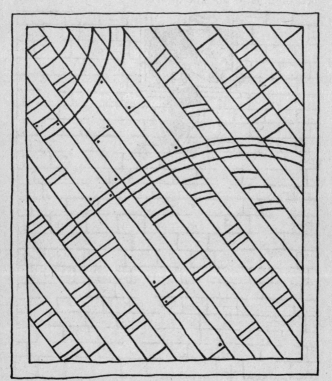

Midnight Escape

William has been sent to his bedroom in disgrace. The other Outlaws want him to come to their midnight feast at the barn, so William escapes from his bedroom. How does he do it?

ROBIN HOOD AND HIS OUTLAWS!

Violet Elizabeth Bott's father has a proper archery set. The Outlaws all tried it out, and they all managed to hit the target. Which Outlaw scored the most points?

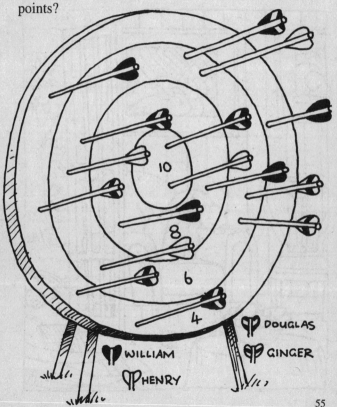

Outlaws are Best

The Outlaws would like to be pirates more than anything else. But they can't find their weapons. Their parents have hidden them. Can you find all 9?

Answers

5 William Finds Hidden Treasure

8 William The Cook

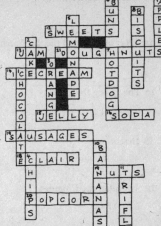

7 The Very Odd Monster

10 The Big Fight

12 The Midnight Feast

D

14 The Outlaws and the Big Catch

D

16 The Fancy Dress Party

6 pairs

18 Detention

45. 45. 45. 46

19 Sweeping the Chimney

B C D F G

20 The Outlaws Build a Bike

D

22 Outlaw Band

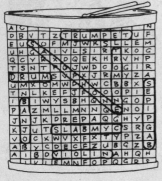

23 Deadly Enemies

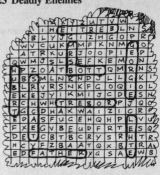

25 The Hidden Weapons

26 William the Detective

G

58

28 The Outlaws' Favourite Things

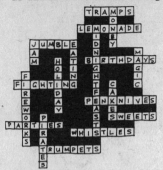

38 Never Play With Matches

32 All the Fun of the Fair

20p 17p 16p 13p 19p or

20p 17p 25p 13p 10p

35 Greedy Hubert

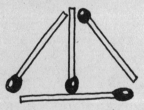

36 Bathing Jumble

A

39 Foreigners

Down With School

40 Down with School

The hidden word is ICE CREAM

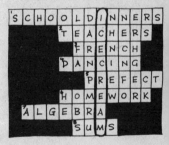

44 William and the Tea-Party.

48 William the Photographer

50 The Outlaws' Barn

52 Henry's Disguise

A

55 Robin Hood and his Outlaws.

Henry

56 Outlaws are Best

Richmal Crompton's
WILLIAM BOOKS

* * * * * *

Just William's World - a pictorial map
by Gillian Clements and Kenneth Waller

* * * * * *

School is a Waste of Time!
by William Brown (and Richmal Crompton)

* * * * * *

Other Outlaws Club books you will enjoy:

JUST - WILLIAM'S

TRICKS: Be a magician! Amaze your friends!
CODES: Master codes and become a spy!
PLAYS: Be a great actor! Play Macbeth and
defeat Captain Hook!

William invites you!

Join my club and becum a nOutlaw William Brown

You can join the new Outlaws Club!

You will receive
a special Outlaws wallet
containing the new Outlaws badge, the club rules
and your membership card
and
a pad for secret messages, a club pencil
and a letter from William giving you the
secret password

To join the club send £2.50 and a letter with your name
and address, written in block capitals, telling us you want to
join the Outlaws to:

The Outlaws Club
Children's Marketing Department
MACMILLAN CHILDREN'S BOOKS
18-21 Cavaye Place
London SW10 9PG

You must live in the United Kingdom or the Republic of Ireland
in order to join.